SUN, SUN

written by **Brad Gray**

illustrated by **Alexandra Tillard**

For Denyon, my enthusiastic beach nut. – B.G.

For my two favorite characters, Aaron and Oliver. – A.T.

Sun, Sun,
Where have you been?
We've missed you here
In West Michigan!

The winter was long,
The spring was dreary—
So glad you came back
To make our lives cheery.

With your warm rays
It's time to reach
For suits and sand toys,
As we head to the beach!

Our excitement swells
Leaving the parking lot.
We stroll down the boardwalk
Looking for a great spot!

Close to the water
We claim our beach space.
The sunscreen is applied
From our toes to our face.

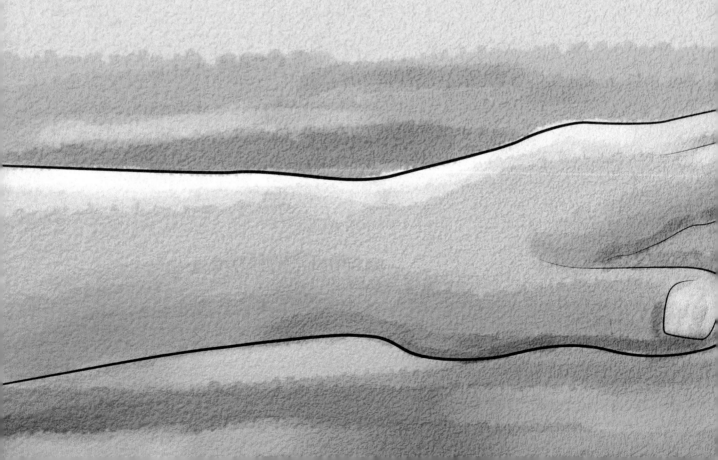

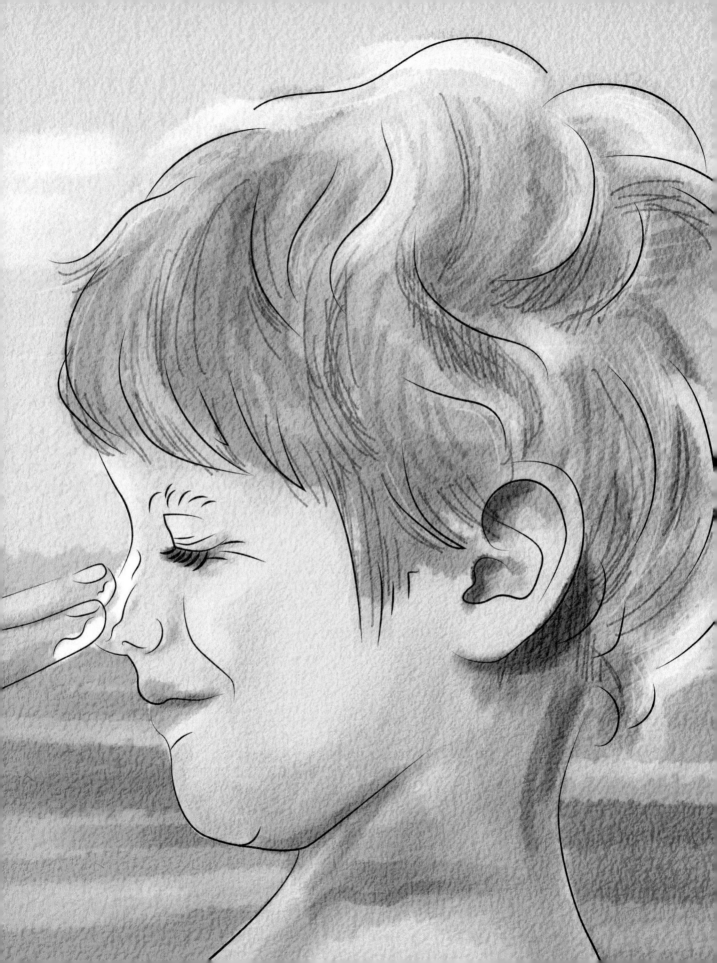

We race into the water:
Oh my! It's chilly!
But we don't care,
We splash and act silly.

With buckets and shovels
We craft a sand land,
Of castles and pyramids
And pits that are grand.

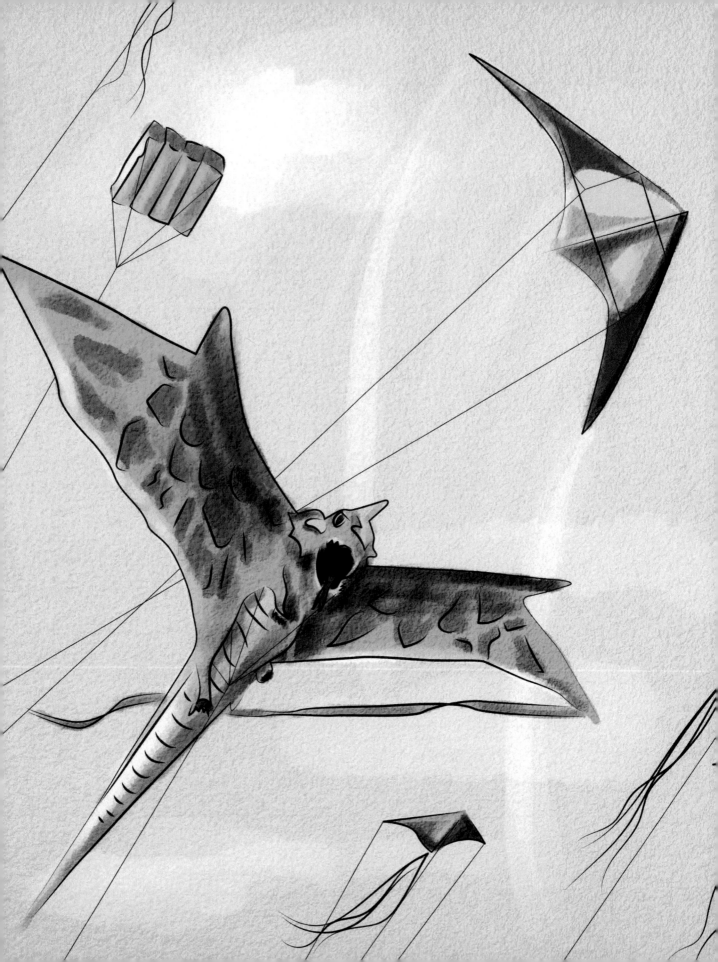

Sprawled out on our backs,
We take in the kite view
Of dragons and butterflies,
And ones that spin too!

It's time for a treat,
And only one will suffice.
We'll take the ice cream—
You can keep your shaved ice!

With hearts full of gratitude
We recall today's fun
Was largely made possible
By you, a self-giving sun.

You say your goodnight
With a dazzling light show
Of breathtaking colors
That leaves our hearts aglow.

Thank you so much for purchasing this book! We had so much fun creating this book for you to enjoy. We trust you had as much fun reading it as we did creating it.

If you liked this story, we'd be most grateful if you'd help us out by taking a few moments and leaving us a review with the retailer where you bought this book. Thank you so much!

As a FREE BONUS to purchasing this book, for a limited time, we'd like to gift you all eleven illustrations in this book as coloring book pages for you and your loved ones to add your own color and creativity to.

Peace, love and duckies,

Brad Gray and Alexandra Tillard

Get your FREE coloring book at:

walkingthetext.com/sun-sun-coloring-book

Made in the USA
Monee, IL
23 January 2020